The Fairies of Starshine Meadow

✱ ✱ ✱ ⚘

Ivy and the
Fantastic Friend

Collect all the sparkling adventures of
The Fairies of Starshine Meadow!

The Fairies of Starshine Meadow

Ivy and the Fantastic Friend

Kate Bloom and Emma Pack

stripes

Fairy Lore

In Starshine Meadow, a grassy dell,
Shimmering fairies flutter and dwell.
Throughout the seasons they nurture and nourish,
Helping the plants and flowers to flourish.

To grant humans' wishes is the fairies' delight,
Spreading magic and happiness in day- and moonlight.
But to human beings, they must remain unseen,
So says their ruler, the Dandelion Queen.

When a wish has been made the fairies must speed,
Back to the meadow to start their good deed.
There they must seek the queen's permission,
Before setting off on their wish-granting mission.

And when the queen has agreed, wait they must,
For a sprinkling of her special wish-dust.
Then off they fly to help those who call,
Spreading their magic to one and all.

When a wish is made and fairies are near,
You can be certain that they will hear.
They'll work their magic to make a dream come true,
And leave a special fairy charm just for you!

For fairies love the secret work they do,
And a fairy promise is always true.
So next time you're lonely or full of woe,
Call on the fairies of Starshine Meadow!

Taylor's Riding School

Starshine Meadow

Moonbeam Wood

← To the Next Village

The Village of
GREENTHORN

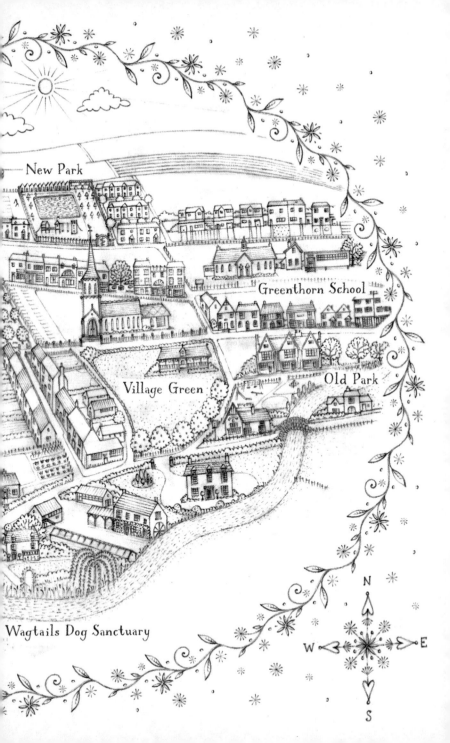

To Bailei - darling, magical little girl.
KB

To Maisie and George - you two are my wish come true!
EP

STRIPES PUBLISHING
An imprint of Magi Publications
1 The Coda Centre, 189 Munster Road, London SW6 6AW

A paperback original
First published in Great Britain in 2006

Characters created by Emma Pack
Text copyright © Susan Bentley, 2006
Illustrations copyright © Emma Pack, 2006

ISBN-10: 1-84715-000-4
ISBN-13: 978-1-84715-000-4

A CIP catalogue record for this book is available
from the British Library.

Printed and bound in Belgium by Proost

2 4 6 8 10 9 7 5 3 1

Chapter One

"What a lovely spring day!" cried Ivy. She fluttered into the garden behind Bramble Cottage and hovered above a patch of snowdrops. They shivered and tinkled with a sound like tiny bells as Ivy fanned them with her wings.

"The whole garden's coming to life," she beamed.

A hedgehog and her
two babies snuffled
a greeting, and Ivy
waved to them cheerily.
She felt like the luckiest fairy in the
whole of Starshine Meadow. From
the tips of her sparkly green wings to
the glittery hem of her dress she
glowed with happiness.

Everything in the garden behind
the empty cottage was coming to life.
Ivy had discovered the garden one
winter's morning, and she came here
often to make sure all the flowers
grew strong and healthy for when the
garden had a new owner. She knew
just which buds were about to burst
and which shy, delicate blossoms
needed a whisper of encouragement.

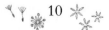

Today it felt extra magical in the garden, because she'd invited her three best friends to come with her.

"Rose! Belle! Daisy!" Ivy called.

There was a flash of mixed pink and blue light and two fairies whooshed up from the overgrown lawn, waving.

"It's beautiful!" cried Rose. "You can see the flowers are happy!" Rose had long, flowing, brown hair to her waist. Her wings were sugar pink and she wore a dress of pink rose petals. "Mmm. The roses smell delicious!" she said, sniffing deeply.

"It all looks wonderful. You've worked so hard. I can see why you like coming here so much, Ivy!" said Bluebell. She had springy dark hair, and her dress had misty blue skirts.

"Oooh! Look at those foxgloves. They would make a fabulous hat!"

Ivy beamed delightedly at her friends. "Where's Daisy?"

Ivy, Rose and Bluebell looked around.

"There she is!" Ivy glimpsed a spot of bright yellow light darting busily round a patch of purple clover. "Hey, Daisy! What are you doing?"

"Did someone call me?" a sunny voice answered.

Daisy flew into the air on shimmering, bright yellow wings. She zoomed over in a flurry of yellow and white skirts, her blonde hair tied in two neat bunches, and hovered next to her friends.

"I was collecting nectar," Daisy said excitedly, patting her acorn bag, which was slung over one shoulder. "I've promised to make clover cordial for the Spring Ball! It's going to be brilliant!"

The ball was being held in the branches of the great oak tree. The tree stood in a corner of Starshine Meadow, a field full of wild flowers just outside Greenthorn village. Ivy lived in the meadow with all the other fairies, and the oak was home to the fairies' Dandelion Queen.

"Clover cordial sounds delicious," said Rose. "I'm working on a new poem, but it's not quite right yet."

"I'm going to make some special lanterns to decorate the tree," Ivy said.

"And I'm making us all pretty crowns to go with our best gowns," Bluebell added.

Ivy beamed at her friends. They were all so clever in different ways.

"Lots of our fairy cousins will be coming," Daisy said. "I'm so looking forward to seeing them. There's not much time to get everything ready. It's only three days away…"

"Yes – we know!" Ivy, Rose and Bluebell sang out quickly.

Daisy's face turned as pink as crab-apple jelly. "Sorry!" she said with a wide grin. "I know I can get a bit carried away. I'm just so excited about the ball."

Rose flew across and gave Daisy a hug. "Don't be sorry. We love you just the way you are," she said sweetly.

"And that's having brilliant ideas and more energy than the three of us put together!" Ivy exclaimed, as she flew into the air. "Come on, everyone! The apple blossom is just opening."

With a whirring of fairy wings, her three friends flew after her.

Ivy led them under a crumbling wooden archway to the old apple tree, which overlooked the drive in front of the empty cottage. She floated down and sat on a branch. First Daisy, then Rose and Bluebell landed beside her.

"You're right about this apple blossom!" exclaimed Belle, cupping a fragrant pink and white flower in her tiny hands. "It smells just—"

Suddenly a loud rumbling noise came from the lane behind the tall hedge. The apple tree's branches trembled.

"Oh!" Ivy gasped, clutching Rose to steady herself.

"What's happening?" Belle fluttered into the air in alarm.

"It's a thunderstorm!" Daisy shrieked dramatically, throwing herself flat along the branch.

Chapter Two

Ivy's heart beat fast. She peeped round the side of Rose at the big red car as it turned into the drive. It was followed by an enormous lorry, with *Blake's Speedy Removals* written on the side.

She gave a relieved laugh. "You can get up now, Daisy. It isn't a thunderstorm."

The noisy lorry chugged to a
halt. A big puff of black smoke rose
from somewhere at the back of it.

"Phew – car fumes!" Daisy
spluttered, screwing up her tiny face.
"Ah … ah choo! Ah choo!"

Belle floated down to pat Daisy on the back. "Bless you!" she said, giggling.

"Hush, you two!" Rose whispered urgently. "Hurry! We'd better hide," she said, steering Ivy behind some blossom.

Daisy and Bluebell quickly joined them.

It was an important fairy law that fairies must never be seen by humans. All the fairies in Starshine Meadow took this law very seriously. The Dandelion Queen was very unhappy with any fairy who broke this rule, even if it was by accident. She had to make some special magic dust to sprinkle on the human so they forgot everything they had seen.

"Look! Someone's getting out of the car. It looks as if Bramble Cottage has a new family to look after it." Ivy peeped round a cluster of petals as a man, a woman and a girl appeared. She felt very excited. What would the family moving into Bramble Cottage think of their garden? She hoped they'd love it as much as she did.

Ivy watched the girl. She looked about eight. She had big, sad blue eyes and long fair hair, and her hands were folded tightly across her chest.

The woman had a kind face and curly dark hair. "Here we are at last! Bramble Cottage!" she said, slamming the car door.

"Home to the Martin family! Just smell that fresh country air!" said the man, who was tall and had sandy hair. "Well, Jessica. What do you think of your new home?"

"It's ... er ... very nice." Jessica flicked back her hair and glanced at the peeling paint, cobwebs and dusty windows. "But it's a bit scruffy, isn't it?"

Mrs Martin smiled. "Bramble Cottage is over two hundred years old! And it's been empty for ages. There's nothing wrong that a bit of elbow grease and a coat of paint won't fix!"

"I s'pose so," Jessica said, hunching her shoulders.

"What a pretty girl! I like her," Rose whispered to Ivy. "She doesn't look very happy though, does she?"

"No," Ivy agreed, starting to feel worried. If Jessica didn't like Bramble Cottage she might not like the garden either.

"There's a huge garden. Why don't you go and have a look around, while we start settling in?" Mrs Martin suggested to her daughter.

"That's a good idea, Jess," Mr Martin agreed. "And then we'll help you unpack and put up your posters in your new bedroom. We could even get some new ones, if you like?"

"No!" Jessica burst out. "I mean … thanks, but I'll keep my old ones." She lowered her voice, but Ivy heard her say quietly, "They might make my horrible new bedroom feel more like home."

Two men had got out of the removal truck. They rolled up the back to reveal furniture covered in

bubble-wrap and lots of cardboard
boxes. Jessica took one look and
turned to open the garden gate.

"Don't go out of the garden, will
you? See you later!" her mum called.

"Don't count on it." Jessica
thrust her hands in her pockets and
trudged down the path.

"Oh, dear." Rose's gentle face clouded with sadness. "Jessica doesn't seem very happy to be here at all!"

"I'm going after her!" said Ivy, already fluttering down and skimming along the top of the hedge.

Rose, Daisy and Bluebell followed. "Wait for us…"

"This garden is huge!" Jessica gazed at the wooden arch and the flowerbeds that were choked with weeds. She gradually wove her way past the uncut lawns and overgrown vegetable plot, and made her way down to the bottom of the garden.

Here there were pretty snowdrops and primroses in the grass. Moss covered the stones around a small pond and ferns and bluebells grew in the damp and shady places under the trees.

Ivy and Rose watched her, peeping out from behind some buttercups. Daisy and Bluebell hid themselves behind a tall nettle. Ivy held her breath. *Please let Jessica like the garden,* she thought.

28

"Wow!" Jessica whispered, sinking on to a moss-covered log. "It's really lovely down here. It's like having a secret magical place all to myself." She looked towards the bluebells that seemed to shine like jewels in the grass. "I just bet there are fairies here!"

"She doesn't know how right she is!" said Ivy. Bluebell, Rose and Daisy bit back delighted laughter.

Jessica gave a deep sigh. "If only Laura was here," she said in a small, sad voice. "We could have had great fun playing games and hunting for

 29

fairies. But what's the use of having a brilliant garden, if there's no one to play with? I don't know anyone round here." Silent tears ran down her face. "I wish…"

There was a moment of complete silence. Time seemed to stand still for Ivy. She glanced across at Rose, Belle and Daisy. They were all wide-eyed and holding their breath. Ivy's heart gave an odd little skip as she turned back to look at Jessica.

Something very special was about to happen.

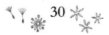

*I WISH I COULD MAKE
A WONDERFUL NEW
BEST FRIEND!*

Chapter Three

"I wish ... I could make a wonderful new best friend," Jessica said, as she brushed a tear from her eye.

Ivy watched with delight as a little cloud of sparkling mist appeared above Jessica's head. Letters formed out of the mist and the wish-words hung there as plain as the stripes on a wasp.

Ivy fluttered her wings with excitement and only just stopped herself from flying right into view. Now she could help Jessica.

"Don't worry, Jessica. I'm going to make your wish come true!" Ivy promised as she took a spider-silk net from a tiny bag at her waist.

Jessica glanced down to where Ivy, Belle, Rose and Daisy were hiding, as if she might have heard something. But then she got up and headed slowly back towards Bramble Cottage.

As soon as Jessica was out of sight, the fairies flew out of their hiding place, beaming excitedly.

"You've got a wish, Ivy!" said Rose. "Lucky you!"

"We'll help you collect it and take it to the Dandelion Queen," said Daisy. "Oh, I do hope she lets you grant the wish!"

Holding one corner of the net each, they gathered up all the sparkling letters.

"Ready everyone? Off we go!" said Ivy. Clutching the net, she led the way back to Starshine Meadow.

The great oak in the corner of the meadow had a thick, twisted trunk and huge spreading branches. From high up near the top came a sound, like a silvery bell.

"Listen! It's the Dandelion Queen's clock striking inside the tree. It's telling everyone about the wish," said Belle.

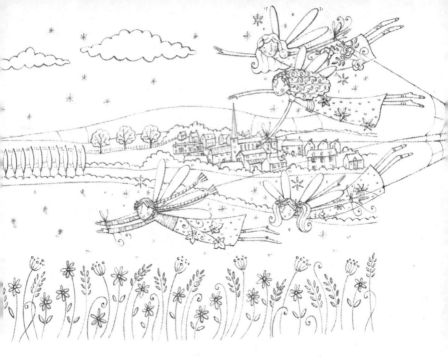

"We'll wait here while you collect your wand," said Rose.

Ivy flew over to her bed and grabbed her wand. Then she and her friends hurried over to the tree. Each one of the oak's leaves glittered with magical fairy light, but to human beings it looked just like sunlight shining through the branches.

"Look, all the fairies are gathering to hear about the wish," Rose added excitedly.

Ivy saw that Rose was right. Fairies clustered along all the oak's lower branches. Rose, Belle and Daisy swooped down and squeezed into a space. Rose waved at her friend. "Good luck, Ivy," she called.

Feeling a little nervous, Ivy flew down and landed next to a tiny arch at the base of the trunk.

There was a sound of tinkling bells and the Dandelion Queen stepped through the arch. She wore a splendid golden petal gown and her crown was a curling dandelion bud. Her silver blonde hair streamed down her back in a mass of spiral curls.

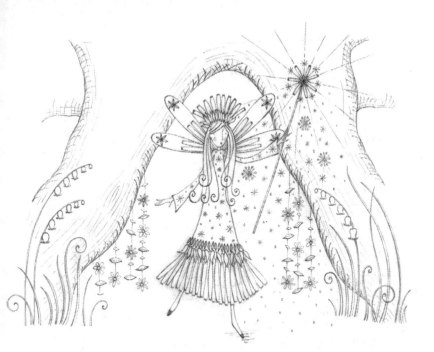

"Ah, Ivy. I see you have already collected the wish," the queen said warmly.

"Yes, Your Majesty," Ivy replied. "It was made by a girl called Jessica Martin. She's just moved into Bramble Cottage, where I have been looking after the garden. She has wished to make a new best friend."

"What a wonderful wish! And I'm sure you'll find a lovely way to grant it," said the Dandelion Queen. "Remember, Ivy, that good magic helps everyone. So the wish may come true in ways you do not expect."

"Thank you. I'll remember that," Ivy promised.

The Dandelion Queen gave a pleased smile. "Hold out your wand."

Ivy did so. The queen shook her dandelion wand and a big spray of wish-dust shot towards Ivy's green, star-tipped wand. It glittered with the tiniest, sweetest dandelion seeds. "Use this magic well. Its power will start to fade after the full moon on the night of the Spring Ball," the queen explained.

"Thank you, Your Majesty." Ivy held her wand tightly. Its glowing tip seemed to shimmer with excitement.

All the other fairies cheered and waved. "Good luck, Ivy!" they called.

Ivy waved back. The Spring Ball was only three days away. She had until then to make Jessica's wish come true. She took off across Starshine Meadow, and hovered in the air above a patch of pink clover.

Rose, Belle and Daisy flew after her.

"Have you thought about how you're going to grant Jessica's wish?" Belle asked eagerly.

"I think I'm going to have to persuade Jessica to go exploring," said Ivy. "She'll never meet anyone if she stays at Bramble Cottage. But I'm not quite sure yet!"

"Why don't you sleep on it?" Belle suggested. "Sometimes brilliant ideas come in dreams. And remember, we're here to help too."

"I will – and thanks! I'll see you all tomorrow."

Chapter Four

Next morning, bright and early, Ivy
flew out of her cosy bed under the
ivy plant and went to find her
friends. The first place she looked
was under the wild rose bush. Rose
was sitting in her nest-like bed with
its canopy of pink spider-silk. Daisy
and Belle were already there, leaning
against the rose-petal cushions.

"Hello, Ivy," they chorused.

"Did you have sweet dreams?" asked Rose.

Ivy floated down and sat beside them. "No!" she laughed. "I've hardly slept, I'm so excited."

"Me too! And I've had a really good idea for granting Jessica's wish," Daisy burst out. "You sprinkle wish-dust on a whole class of schoolgirls, so they come round to Jessica's house! And she makes friends with loads of people all at once. Brilliant, isn't it?"

Ivy put her head on one side. "I'm not sure that would work, Daisy. Wouldn't that be making people do things against their will?" she asked tactfully.

"Oh, yes. I hadn't thought of that." Daisy's face fell as she spotted the flaw in her plan. "That's against fairy law, isn't it?"

"Daisy's right in one way though. Jessica needs to meet lots of people, if she's to make a new best friend," Rose pointed out.

"That's true," said Belle. "Have you had any ideas about how to get Jessica exploring?"

"Not exactly," said Ivy. "That's why I thought I might fly over to Bramble Cottage and see what's

43

nearby. Are you coming?" Her wings flashed as she whooshed up through the rose bush.

Belle, Daisy and Rose fluttered up after her. "Hey! Wait for us!"

Ivy flew a little way ahead of her friends. She saw some shops and a school with children in the playground, but nothing gave her an idea.

But as she drifted over a hedgerow, she spotted some girls riding ponies down a lane near Bramble Cottage.

The riders were chatting and laughing and really enjoying themselves. Ivy watched them turn into a gateway in front of a big house. There was a sign outside that read *Taylor's Riding Stables*.

"That's it!" Ivy exclaimed, coming to a sudden halt, so that Rose, Belle and Daisy banged into each other. "I know how to help Jessica!"

"You do? Oh, good!" Daisy shook out her crumpled wing.

Ivy pointed to the riding school. "All girls love ponies, don't they? If I let Jessica know about these stables, she's bound to want riding lessons. And then she'll meet lots of girls and make a new best friend."

"What a good idea," Rose said. "And those girls looked about the same age as Jessica, too."

"But how are you going to tell Jessica about the riding school?" Belle asked.

Ivy thought hard. "I'll make an invitation, offering her a free riding lesson and deliver it to Bramble Cottage."

"Brilliant!" Daisy said.

Ivy floated down and picked a leaf from a bush in the hedgerow. She tapped it with her wand, and whispered,

Wishes big and wishes small,
With my wand I'll grant them all!

There was a bright golden flash and the leaf turned into a smart invitation made of white card. It had a crinkly gold edge and there was a tiny picture of a horse in one corner. Rose, Belle and Daisy crowded round to read the glittery, gold writing.

To Miss Jessica Martin

As a welcome to the village, you are invited to come to

TAYLOR'S RIDING STABLES

for a free lesson.

No need to phone. Just turn up.

"Perfect!" said Rose, looking impressed. "Jessica won't be able to resist that."

"But won't the stables think it's strange when Jessica just turns up?" asked Belle. "Won't they be puzzled by the invitation?"

Ivy smiled. "Remember what the Dandelion Queen tells us? Good magic will always find a way. We have to trust it. Come on!"

After checking that the coast was clear, the four friends flew down and placed the card on the front doormat outside Bramble Cottage.

"I'll come back tomorrow to see if it's worked," Ivy said.

"I'm sure it will. It's a fabulous idea!" Daisy enthused.

"I must get back to Starshine Meadow now," said Bellle. "I've only made one crown for the ball, so far."

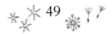

49

"And I need to find my recipe for clover cordial. I'm sure it was under my pillow…" Daisy murmured, nibbling her nails.

"I'm still working on my poem," Rose said. "What about you, Ivy? Are you coming back with us?"

Ivy hadn't even started her flower-bud lanterns, but she couldn't resist going to check on Bramble Cottage's garden. She shook her head. "I'm just going to see how the garden's doing."

"Do you want us to come with you?" her friends asked.

Ivy smiled. "Thanks, but you've all got lots to do. I'll see you back at Starshine Meadow," she called as they flew off.

Ivy fluttered past the old apple tree and the wooden archway. In the back garden, Mrs Martin was sweeping up cut grass from beside the path. Mr Martin was down at the bottom of the garden, raking up a pile of plants.

"Oh," Ivy gasped, her face crumpling with dismay.

Some of the flowerbeds had already been grassed over. And it looked as if the Martins were going to make the wildlife area into lawn too. Where would the hedgehog and her babies live then? And what would happen to the frogs in the pond and the robins and blue tits that were nesting nearby?

Ivy's wings drooped. She had to do something, right away!

Jessica had seemed to like the wildlife area. Maybe she didn't know that it was in danger. Ivy flew up high and spotted Jessica straightaway, sitting reading a magazine on the back doorstep.

While Mr Martin's back was
turned, Ivy flew down and quickly
gathered an armful of petals from the
pulled-up plants. Then she sprinkled
them in a zigzag
trail up to the
back door.

Jessica didn't notice the tiny fairy
fly into the hanging basket above her
and hide behind a pansy. Taking
careful aim, Ivy tossed a big handful
of petals over the side of the basket.

53

"Oh!" Jessica looked up in surprise, as pretty petals fluttered all around her. She stood up to brush them off and spotted the trail Ivy had left. "That's strange. I wonder how those got blown into a pattern like that. It's like a magic message!"

Jessica began following the trail down to where her dad was working. Ivy fluttered along behind her and hid in a nearby bush to watch.

"Dad! What are you doing?"
cried Jessica, as soon as she saw the
large heap of plants.

"Oh, these are just weeds. It'll
look much tidier with more grass,"
Mr Martin said.

"But I like the garden how it is!"
Jessica burst out. "Especially the wild
part at the bottom."

Her dad frowned. "I'd planned to dig that up and put down some paving, so that we can have barbeques. Wouldn't you like that better?"

Jessica looked horrified. "No! I'd hate it. This is a really special place. I saw a bird's nest down here and there's frogspawn in the pond. Please let's leave it as it is."

"It does seem a shame to disturb the wildlife..." her dad said as he stroked his chin.

"Please, please can the wild garden be my own little patch? I'll look after it, I promise," Jessica pleaded.

"I didn't think you'd want to be bothered with the garden," her dad

said, sounding surprised. "But okay.
I suppose the barbeque can go
somewhere else."

"Thanks, Dad!" Jessica leaped
forward and gave him a hug. "I'm
going to love having my own little
garden!"

Ivy felt a warm happy glow. The wildlife area was safe. Now all she had to do was make sure Jessica found the invitation. She flew back to Starshine Meadow, full of enthusiasm for making her lanterns.

Chapter Five

"Stop wriggling, Ivy!" Belle grumbled the next morning, as she tried to get Ivy to try on her crown.

"Sorry!" Ivy said. She was impatient to go and see if Jessica had gone to claim her riding lesson. Was the magic starting to work? "Thank you, Belle. It's beautiful. I love the little crocus-petal stars."

Belle beamed at her. "Do you really like it? It's taken me ages."

"I love my crown too. You're so clever," said Rose, admiring the rose petals and fern flowers on her crown. "Has anyone seen Daisy?"

Belle chuckled. "Haven't you noticed all the fairies with screwed up faces? Daisy's busy with her cordial and she's been asking everyone to try it. It's still a bit sour!"

"I'm sure she'll get it right in time for the party," Rose said with a grin.

Ivy glanced at the big basket of finished lanterns. She had made about fifty, but there was still a big pile of buds to be coaxed into shape.

"Why did I say I'd make all these?" she sighed.

"Why don't I do some for you?"
Belle offered. "It's hopeless trying to
get Daisy to try on her crown. I can't
even catch her!"

Ivy laughed. "Thanks, Belle.
Then I can go and see Jessica."

"If Belle's staying here, I'll come
with you," Rose said. "I've
half finished my
poem. Do you
want to hear it?"

Ivy and Belle
nodded as Rose
began to recite.

Moonlight glistens on us all,
As we gather for the Spring Ball.
Fairy friends bring gifts to share,
And dance and sing in the soft night air.

"That's really lovely, Rose," Ivy enthused.

"And it's just perfect for the opening of the Spring Ball," Belle said with a smile.

Rose flushed pink with pleasure. "Thank you! I have one more verse to write, but I'm so glad you like it! See you later, Belle!" She took Ivy's hand and they flew off together to Taylor's Riding Stables.

As soon as they got there they spotted Jessica and her mum in the stableyard, talking to a man in a tweed cap.

"It looks as if your invitation has worked," Rose whispered. They tucked themselves behind a gatepost and listened.

"Thank you for the offer of a free riding lesson," Mrs Martin was saying. "Jessica's quite scared of horses, so would it be all right if she just had a look round the stables?"

Mr Taylor took off his cap and scratched his head. "I'm afraid I don't know anything about free lessons," he said, staring at the invitation. "It must be something to do with my wife or daughter. And we're closed today. I'm sorry."

"Come on, Mum. Let's go home.
We must have made a mistake,"
Jessica said, looking
embarrassed.

"Oh no! Jessica's afraid of horses!
And the riding stables are closed,"
Ivy whispered anxiously to Rose.
"My idea wasn't very good after all!"

"Wait and see," Rose said
calmly. "Remember what the
Dandelion Queen said. Things often
work out in ways you don't expect."

Ivy nodded, hoping Rose was right.

"Oh, dear. That's a pity. Well, thanks anyway." Mrs Martin turned to go.

"Just a minute," said Mr Taylor. "Would Jessica fancy helping my daughter Amy muck out the ponies? I know it's not quite what you had in mind, but I know Amy would be glad of the help and it might help her to get used to the ponies. And Amy could show her around afterwards."

Mrs Martin looked at Jessica. "What do you think?"

Jessica shrugged. "I don't mind."

Mr Taylor smiled. "That's settled then. Amy, come and say hello to our new neighbours," he called out.

A girl who looked about nine years old came out of the stables holding a rake. She had short brown hair and a friendly smile and was wearing jeans tucked into wellies.

"Amy, this is Jessica. She and her parents have just moved into Bramble Cottage," Mr Taylor explained. "She's not very used to horses, but she's offered to give you a hand."

Jessica turned a panicky face to her mum. "I'm not sure…"

"Just give it a try," Mrs Martin said. "Amy will look after you."

Amy nodded and smiled at Jessica. "Don't worry. You'll be fine. Would you like to come and meet the ponies?" she said, turning towards the stables. "They're all real sweeties. We have Peaches, Brownie, Tess, Meg, Patch and Sally. Sally's my pony," she said proudly.

"Are … are they very big?" Jessica murmured, hanging back. She looked very pale.

"Jessica looks terrified," Rose whispered.

Ivy bit her lip. "How can I make her feel less scared?"

"We could ask the ponies to be really friendly to her," Rose suggested.

Ivy nodded. "Good idea. But she's too scared even to go into the stables. If only there was some way to make her *see* that the ponies won't hurt her." Suddenly her face lit up. "I know what to do!"

She waved her wand. There was a golden flash and a shower of sparkly dust shot out, as she whispered the words,

Wishes big and wishes small,
With my wand I'll grant them all!

A pair of sparkly spectacles floated straight over to Jessica and settled on her nose.

"Now everything in the stables will look all soft and glowing. She won't be able to resist going inside to have a look!" Ivy said.

Rose smiled. "Brilliant!"

Jessica stood there in her invisible glasses. She blinked hard as she peered in through the doorway. Her tense face relaxed, and she started to smile as she took one slow step forward, and then another.

Ivy beamed at Rose. The magic spectacles were working.

"Now it's time to talk to the ponies," Ivy whispered, and she whooshed into the stables through a tiny window. Rose flew in after her and settled herself on a rafter.

Ivy floated down and hovered by the nearest pony's ear. "Will you please be very friendly to Jessica?" she whispered. She flew to each pony in turn and asked the same thing. As they listened, each one twitched its ears and bowed its head.

Ivy sat down beside Rose, just as Jessica and Amy reached the ponies. She could see the magic glasses twinkling with pale-pink light.

The ponies all moved together. They dipped their heads and whinnied a soft welcome, blinking at Jessica with soft dark eyes. As Jessica smiled with delight, the nearest pony stretched forward and nuzzled her arm very gently.

Amy's jaw dropped. "I've never seen the ponies act like that before! It's like they're all saying hello to you! And look at Peaches – she's dying to make friends!"

"Really?" Jessica smiled from ear to ear. She reached towards Peaches and stroked her nose. "Hi, Peaches."

With a tiny *Pop!* which only Ivy and Rose could hear, the magic glasses disappeared.

Jessica rubbed her eyes. She blinked again as the soft rosy glow faded.

Ivy and Rose held their breath. Would Jessica panic now that she could see the ponies properly?

Jessica seemed to stiffen, but then a slow smile spread over her face. "I can't believe I'm actually stroking a pony," she said as she patted Peaches' velvety nose.

Ivy grinned at Rose. "The glasses worked. They gave Jessica confidence to try something new. Now she doesn't need them any more!"

"I thought you said you were nervous?" Amy said to Jessica with a grin. "You're a natural with ponies!"

Jessica shook her head. "This is really weird. I've always been terrified of ponies. But it feels like magic — I can't believe I'm not scared at all!"

Ivy and Rose clapped their hands in silent glee.

After a few more minutes, Jessica turned to Amy. "I could stroke the ponies all day. But shouldn't I be helping you clean the stables?"

"Muck out, you mean? You'll soon see why we call it that!" Amy joked. She found Jessica some spare wellies. "Now all we need to do is grab a couple of rakes!"

Jessica worked hard for the next hour or so. She and Amy forked out the dirty bedding, put down clean straw, and refilled the hay nets.

Finally, Amy straightened up and ran her fingers through her short hair. "All finished. Thanks a lot, Jessica. It's taken me half as long with your help. And it's been fun."

"No problem," Jessica said, grinning. "I loved it. The ponies are gorgeous, especially Peaches."

"Why don't you ask your parents if you can have some lessons?" Amy said.

"I think I might. Could I ride Peaches?" Jessica asked.

Amy nodded. "Of course. And once you get confident enough, we can go out riding together. There are some lovely bridle paths through the woods."

"I'd love that!" said Jessica.

"Before I came here today, I was really missing my old best friend. But today I made two new ones. You and Peaches!"

Amy gave her a brilliant smile. "I've made a new friend today too!"

Ivy and Rose beamed at each other in delight.

"You were right!" Ivy said, giving Rose a hug. "Things can work out in ways you don't expect."

"Yes," Rose answered. "They did for Jessica. With a little help from a friendly fairy and some sparkly wish-dust!"

Chapter Six

The first star shone in the violet sky above Starshine Meadow. The silver disc of the full moon sailed overhead, and the air seemed to hum with excitement.

"It's finally here – the Spring Ball!" Ivy peered down through the oak's branches at the fairies setting out delicious food and drink.

"Could you just hold this lantern while I tie it? That's the last one," Ivy said with relief.

Belle, Rose and Daisy had been helping Ivy to fix them in the tree. "Come on, let's have a look," said Belle. They flew into the meadow and then turned back towards the oak to get the full effect.

"Ooh!" Daisy gasped. "Your lanterns are … are … splendiferous!"

Belle and Rose laughed. Ivy felt proud of her hard work. The lanterns really were fabulous. The oak seemed strung with necklaces of gold jewels shimmering in the twilight.

"Thanks ever so much, all of you. I wouldn't have finished them without your help," Ivy said breathlessly.

"What are friends for?" Belle and Daisy said.

"And you did have more important things on your mind. Like making Jessica's wish come true," Rose said, linking arms.

Ivy smiled warmly at them all. Rose, Belle and Daisy were the best friends any fairy could have.

"Shall we change into our ball gowns? I can't wait to wear my lovely new crown!" Ivy said.

As Ivy, Belle, Daisy and Rose returned to the oak, tinkling fairy music rang out. They held hands as they drifted down on to a branch.

The Dandelion Queen was standing in front of the arch in the hollow trunk. She looked magnificent in a flowing gown of silver and pearl-white, and her crown was a starburst of feathery dandelion seeds.

Fairies lined the oak's branches and floated in the air. The moonlight gleamed on their flashing wings as they hovered with hushed excitement. The music stopped and everyone waited for the Dandelion Queen to open the ball.

"Welcome, fairies!" she said warmly. "Rose will now begin with a special party poem."

Rose flew down and stood next to the queen, in a gown of beautiful rose petals. She took a deep breath.

Moonlight glistens on us all,
As we gather for the Spring Ball.
Fairy friends bring gifts to share,
And dance and sing in the soft night air.

With pretty dresses and sparkling wings,
They talk of wishes and precious things.
It is a time to dance and feast,
Until the sun rises in the east.

All the fairies clapped and cheered. But Bluebell, Ivy and Daisy cheered the loudest. They were so proud of their friend.

The fairy orchestra began to play again and all the fairies danced along the oak's branches. Ivy whirled round and round in her flowing gown of green net. Belle looked pretty in lacy pale blue and Daisy wore wispy cream spider-silk. Their pretty new crowns of moss and petals drew lots of admiring glances.

Everyone had the best time ever. And at the end of the ball, the Dandelion Queen handed out gifts of fairy sweets made from nectar and honeydew. "How are you getting on with Jessica's wish?" she asked Ivy.

"Very well, thank you, Your Majesty." Ivy told the queen about what had happened at the stables.

"Excellent, Ivy! You have helped to make Jessica a very happy girl," said the queen, smiling kindly. Don't forget that the wish-dust will begin to lose its power soon."

"I won't, Your Majesty." Ivy smiled, feeling very happy for Jessica. There was one last thing she needed to do tomorrow, and her friends were going to help her.

The sky was tinged with dawn pink by the time the last fairy lantern went out and all the fairies slipped away to their beds.

"Don't forget we're going to visit Jessica tomorrow," Ivy reminded Rose, Belle and Daisy. And then, tired but happy, she curled up under her cobweb quilt.

The next morning Ivy's tummy fizzed with excitement as she flew towards Bramble Cottage with her friends. As they flew past the neat lawns and the newly trimmed roses, they heard voices coming from the bottom of the garden.

"It's Jessica! And look, Amy's with her!" Ivy exclaimed, drifting down behind a moss-covered stone.

The two girls were sitting on the grass in the wildlife area, chatting.

"I just knew they would be best friends in no time!" Rose said happily.

"...and this is my own patch of garden," Jessica was saying. "Mum and Dad said I could look after it. Aren't these wild flowers pretty?" She lowered her voice. "I'm sure fairies live here."

Belle, Rose and Daisy all looked delighted. Ivy's tiny heart swelled with happiness. Jessica was going to give her garden all the love it needed.

"I bet they do too! It's beautiful. You're so lucky," Amy enthused. "We haven't got much of a garden. Dad says we'd never keep up with it. The stables take up all our time."

Jessica smiled. "You can share mine. You can come here whenever you like."

Amy looked delighted. "Really? That's brilliant. Thanks." She stood up. "Why don't you come over to the stables tomorrow? I can show you how to groom the ponies and we can walk them, if you like."

"I'd love to," Jessica said with a happy smile. She stood up and strolled up the garden with Amy. "I'm starting school in the village on Monday. What class are you in…?" Her voice got fainter as she moved away.

Ivy felt very happy. Her task was almost done. She just had one more thing to do – leave a fairy charm for Jessica.

Daisy, Rose and Belle helped Ivy find a big leaf. Then all together they whispered,

Fairies all will make a charm,
to bring good luck and do no harm!

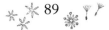

Ivy waved her wand. There was a flash and a final whoosh of sparkly wish-dust shot out and covered the leaf. All the fairies blew gently, and tiny golden writing appeared.

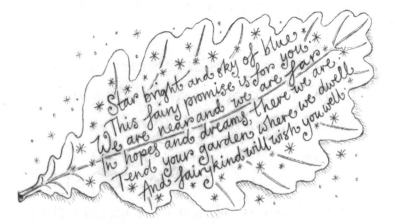

Holding the leaf between them, the fairies flew up to Jessica's open bedroom window. As soon as they had placed the leaf on Jessica's pillow, they heard footsteps hurrying up the stairs.

"Quick, hide! Here she comes!"
whispered Ivy. The fairies zoomed
outside and crouched on the window
sill, peering in.

Jessica spotted the sparkling leaf
at once. "What's this?" she gasped.
Her eyes widened as she picked it up
and read the poem aloud, tracing the
glittering writing with her fingers.

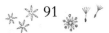

The moment she had finished,
the leaf flew out of her hands and
dissolved into a shower of golden dust.

"Maybe fairies really do live at
the bottom of my garden!" Jessica
whispered, smiling. "And wishes
really can come true!" She ran over
to the window.

Ivy, Rose, Daisy and Belle
whirled round and flew high into the
sky. They glanced back, just for a
second, before setting off for
Starshine Meadow.

Framed in the window, Jessica's
happy, glowing face was as bright as
a fairy lantern.

Belle and the Magic Makeover

"I wish this park could be as good as new."

Fiona's park is full of litter and needs a makeover
fast! Can Belle work her magic and help make
Fiona's wish come true…?

Daisy and the Dazzling Drama

"I wish I could have a bigger part in the play."

Emily is desperate for a larger role in the school
play, but all the parts have been given out.
Can Daisy find a way to help make Emily's
wish come true?

Rose and the Perfect Pet

"I wish I could somehow have a dog."

Neema wants a dog more than anything, but her mum and dad have said no. Can Rose make Neema's wish come true without upsetting her parents…?

And collect the fabulous fairy bookmarks – there's one in every Fairies of Starshine Meadow book!